This book belongs to

....

....

To my very dear friend Neil Mountain, with love
S.J-P.

To my mother, Ella Macnaughton
T.M.

First published in Great Britain in 2005 by Gullane Children's Books
This paperback edition published in 2006 by

Gullane Children's Books
an imprint of Pinwheel Limited
Winchester House, 259-269 Old Marylebone Road,
London NW1 5XJ

1 3 5 7 9 10 8 6 4 2

Text © Susie Jenkin-Pearce 2005
Illustrations © Tina Macnaughton 2005

The right of Susie Jenkin-Pearce and Tina Macnaughton to be identified as the author and illustrator of this work
has been asserted by them in accordance with the Copyright, Designs and Patents Act, 1988.
A CIP record for this title is available from the British Library.

ISBN-13: 978-1-86233-615-5
ISBN-10: 1-86233-615-6

Printed and bound in Singapore

Pugwug and Little

Susie Jenkin-Pearce

Tina Macnaughton

GULLANE
CHILDREN'S BOOKS

Pugwug was out slipping and sliding, when BANG, he bumped into something BIG.

Pugwug just had to know what
all the penguins were looking at.

He bounced . . .

He flapped . . .

He tried diving through a tiny gap . . .

. . . but it was no use.

Eventually, Big Penguin turned around. On his feet there was something large and round.

"Pugwug," said Big Penguin, "meet your new little brother . . . or maybe sister!"

Pugwug was beside himself.
He shrieked with delight.
"Come on, Little," he
yelled, "let's play!"

But Little did not seem to want to play.
In fact, Little did nothing at all.

Pugwug tried to make Little look
more like a brother . . . or sister!

But he made a bit of a mess.
So Big Penguin had to give Little a wash.

"Come on – let's race!" said Pugwug.

"Or . . . let's play catch!" said Pugwug.

"Maybe not . . ." said Big Penguin gently.

Big Penguin
was exhausted!

Suddenly a shout went up
"Danger – seal alert! Penguin in trouble!"

"Pugwug," said Big Penguin gravely,
"look after Little. WATCH, but don't TOUCH!"
Then Big Penguin flapped away as fast as he could.

Pugwug and Little were
all on their own.
Suddenly, Little began
to wobble . . .

and shake
and rock and roll . . .

Pugwug didn't know
what to do . . . !

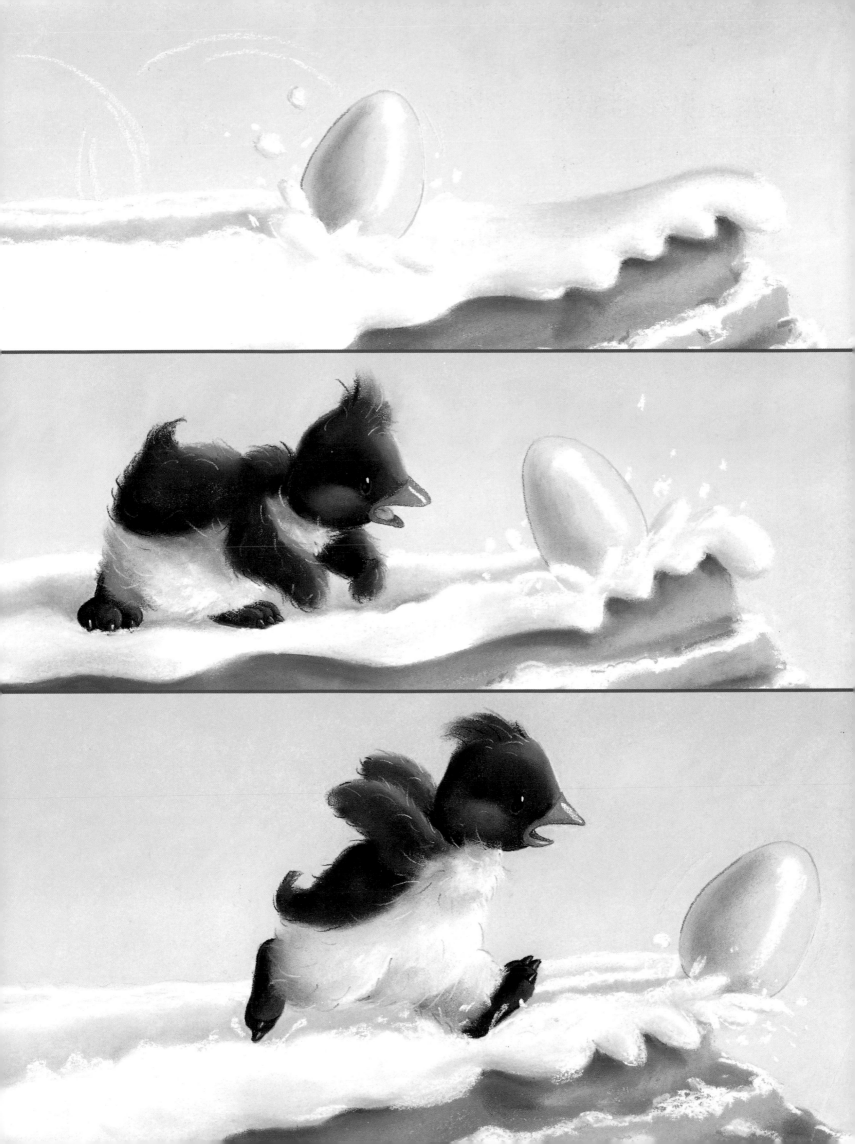

. . . but then he realised he HAD to touch!

Pugwug made
a great dive
and clasped Little
close to him.

AND THEN . . .

When Big Penguin returned, he found
Little snuggled against Pugwug.
"Big Penguin," said Pugwug,
"meet my new baby . . .

. . . sister!"

Other Gullane Children's Books
for you to enjoy . . .

The Lamb-a-roo
Diana Kimpton • Rosalind Beardshaw

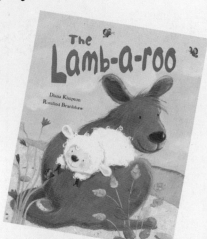

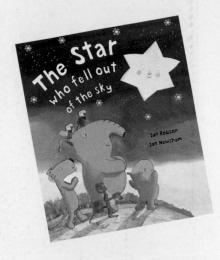

**The Star Who Fell
Out of the Sky**
Ian Robson • Ian Newsham

Stick With Me!
James Croft • Greg Gormley